To Ensign Harry Noel Devlin, U.S.N.R.

THE KNOBBY BOYS TO THE RESCUE

by Wende and Harry Devlin

Parents' Magazine Press

Printed in the United States of America
Library of Congress Catalog Card Number 65-10465

Every afternoon, three noisy and fun-loving friends met to play dominoes and tell fibs. They called themselves the "Knobby Boys" just because they liked the name.

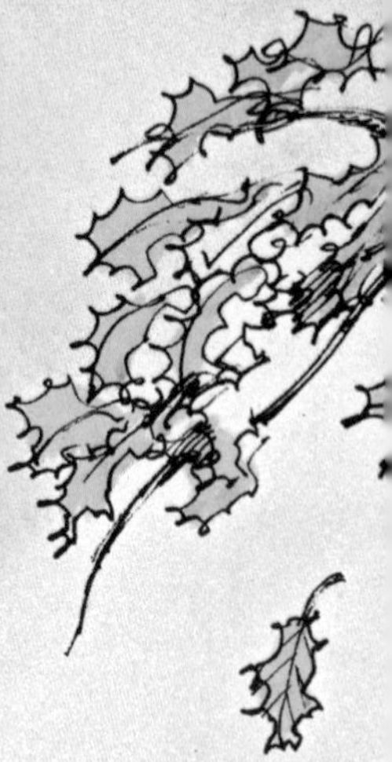

It was a late summer day as they sat around an old tree stump and tasted Raccoon's homemade root beer. Fox was first to hear the sniffling.

"That sounds like sniffling," said Fox. The sniffling grew louder and became a howl.

"Sounds like a howl," squeaked Raccoon.

"More like a bellow," said Crow, as the trees shook.

The Knobby Boys threw down their dominoes and covered their ears. There would be no game for the Boys this day. Cross and grumbling, they followed the howls to Bear Cave.

There, all alone, sat Baby Brown Bear. He was sad, teary-eyed and, oh! so hungry. Between sobs Baby Brown Bear told the Boys that his mother had disappeared.

"She's gone, and I'm a baby bear who is all alone in this world," he sobbed.

Fox stared at Bear. "Great gooseberries! Are you a baby?"

"Mother's precious baby and I'm hungry," said Baby Brown Bear, a tear rolling down his nose.

"Fried feathers! Somebody has to feed a baby," Crow said, shifting from foot to foot, uneasily.

"Well," sighed Fox, "if we are ever going to get back to our dominoes—we'd better begin rounding up some food." So the Knobby Boys went off in all directions and, in time, came back with berries, honey, and a small fish. In one bite, Baby Brown Bear ate it all.

"I'm hungry," he said.

Y

The hours and then the days wore on. The Knobby Boys found that the only way to have any peace was to keep Baby Brown Bear fed—and this they did. And as the bear grew fatter, the Knobby Boys grew thinner and wearier and more desperate.

And still the baby grew. He grew so big Fox had to stand on his toes to feed him. Poor Crow had to fly up to his nose and give him berries.

"Are you still a baby?" Crow asked.

"Mother's precious baby," said Baby Brown Bear.

Now the hills became grey and windswept. The nights were cold and snow began to fall in small, swift flurries.

And as winter drew closer, food became harder to find. Fox's tail began to drag, Crow began to look ruffled, and Raccoon had even darker circles under his eyes.

"It won't be long now before some folks around here take that long nap," Fox winked at Crow. "Bears hibernate, you know—sleep all winter."

But Baby Brown Bear showed no interest in winter napping. He was gay, playful, and hungrier than ever.

"Great gooseberries!" said Fox. "I've got an idea. I'll sing him to sleep with a lullaby.

"Lullaby, winter's here.
Flowers close their sweet eyes.
Froggies sleep,
Fishies sleep . . ."

"And baby bears like to eat," added Baby Brown Bear, as he tickled Fox's whiskers.

Fox sighed in despair. And Baby Brown Bear smiled lovingly at his friend.

Happily, however, things were soon to change.

The Knobby Boys, in their search for food, always kept a hopeful eye open for Baby Brown Bear's mother. And then, one wonderful day, it happened!

Crow saw her!

But what a sorry sight she was—chained to a stake. She was dressed in a ruffled skirt and flowered hat. The old gypsy wagon, nearby, told the story. Mrs. Bear had been caught by the cruel couple who captured animals and trained them for the circus. Crow had heard many stories about them.

Swiftly he circled the clearing and then, straight as crows fly, he flew to his friends and told them the news.

“Great gooseberries!” barked Fox.
“Fried feathers! We’re free,” sobbed Crow.
“Dust off the dominoes,” squeaked Raccoon.
After Fox turned a few paw springs, they sat

down and made their daring plans. They would turn into ghosts, scare the gypsies away, and free Mrs. Bear. Fox was able to borrow some pillowcases from a forest ranger's clothesline.

When the blue of night came, they tucked Baby Brown Bear into his cave and set off on their journey through the woods. Flying from tree to tree, Crow led the way. Over the hills and through the creeks the Knobby Boys scrambled their way to the gypsy hideout.

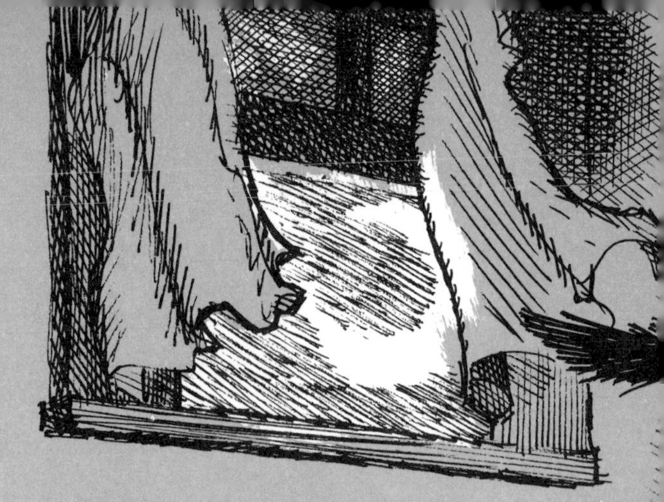

There in the clearing, still chained, slept Mrs. Bear, dreaming of her precious baby. The Knobby Boys plainly heard her sighs.

Crow, silent as the softest breeze, drifted in through the open window of the red wagon. The gypsies were sound asleep in their long red night-caps. Crow's bright eyes searched for a key among beans and buttons and pots and pans.

He poked into a pair of pants that hung on a chair, and his heart almost stopped when the man cried out in his sleep. But, luckily, he slept on, and soon Crow's bright eyes found the key on a nail by the door. With his heart beating wildly, Crow flapped out of the window and screeched, "Now!"

At once Fox and Raccoon began jumping up and down in their ghostly pillowcases. “Boo!” said Fox.

“Squeak!” squeaked Raccoon, who wasn’t quite sure what ghosts were supposed to say.

The sleepy-eyed and frightened gypsies stumbled to the window and saw the awful sight. Two ghosts, leaping and screeching, seemed about to fly through the window.

The terrified couple tore open the door and, in their haste to get away, fell against the wagon's brake.

The wagon began to roll and rattle and pick up speed. Beans, buttons, and biscuits flew out of the window. The back door burst open, and pots and pans and sugar and shoes spilled to the ground. The wild-eyed gypsies clung to the wagon as it thundered down the hill into the very wet pond below.

Crow, Raccoon, and Fox stared in stunned silence. Then they unlocked Mrs. Bear and sank to the ground in exhaustion. It was almost dawn by the time they began the long trip back home with Mrs. Bear.

How wonderful it was to see Mrs. Bear and her precious Baby Brown Bear together again! Mrs. Bear and Baby Brown Bear laughed, cried, hugged, and danced all at once.

Finally, Mrs. Bear remembered her rescuers. "How can I ever thank you?" she said.

The Knobby Boys leaned against one another and, almost in tears, they said, "That baby! Put that baby to sleep!"

Mrs. Bear looked out at the white snow, the black trees, and the silver pond.

"It's time," she said.

The Knobby Boys gathered close, eager to learn the sleep-making magic of a mother bear.

And now the soft and secret bear lullabies began. Crow yawned. Fox, with a foolish grin, closed his eyes and Raccoon snored softly.

With a last look at his sleeping friends, Baby Brown Bear snuggled deep in his mother's arms and dreamed of wild honey and strawberries and plenty of them.

Silent snowflakes fell outside.

The dominoes, hidden in the old tree stump, would have to wait for the warm and wonderful far-off coming of spring.

Harry Devlin